# RED HAI

a Mary MacIntosh novel

# Maureen Anne Meehan

1

# RED HANDS

Copyright © 2024 by Maureen Anne Meehan

ISBN: 979-8-3305-1750-3 (e)

www. maureenmeehanbooks.com

info@maureenmeehan.com

# Dedication

This novel is dedicated to all the missing and murdered Native American women in the United States. This crisis is rooted in a long history of systemic marginalization, lack of proper law enforcement response, and jurisdictional challenges on Native land. Many Indigenous women go missing or are murdered at rates far higher than other populations, and their cases often go unsolved due to jurisdictional issues between tribal, state, and federal authorities, lack of resources, and societal neglect.

In addition to the Red Hands movement, this novel is also dedicated to all of the victims of the Zodiac Killer. The Zodiac Killer remains at large, and the victims and their families will likely never have closure as a result.

Thank you to all my readers and followers for unending support of the craft of fiction and nonfiction.

# Author's Note

Red Hands, a Mary MacIntosh novel, was crafted in honor of all Native American women in the United States who have gone missing or murdered. The "Red Hand" symbolizes the silencing of these women and the crisis of the cause is rooted in a long history of systemic marginalization, lack of proper law enforcement response, and jurisdictional challenges in prosecuting crimes on Native land.

I would like to thank the following people who continue to assist and inspire my craft of fiction and nonfiction. This list is long and I will likely accidentally miss a few people, but I will attempt inclusivity.

Andrea Morrison, Ara Adams, Amelia Pierce, Lora Monroe, Nikki Jones, Raquel Martinez, and all other members of The Eagle Literary, Writers Branding, and Reading Glass Books.

In addition, Jonathan West, Cary Hyden, and Michele Johnson of Latham/Watkins deserve a nod, as well as Ellen Darling of KL Gates.

Alex Abercrombie is an incredible photographer and it is her creation from a photoshoot that creates the back cover photos for my novels of 2024.

And, of course, to family, friends, and readers. This doesn't happen in a bubble. You are all appreciated.

# Table of Contents

# Chapter 1

Walter Leland Cronkite Jr. was an American broadcast journalist who served as anchorman for the CBS Evening News for 19 years, from 1962 to 1981. During the 1960's and 1970's, he was often called "the most trusted man in America" after being so named in an opinion poll. He and Paul Harvey just reported the news. It is not like it is today. Not at all.

But there are some good old school reporters still lurking in the shadows and one of them is Kate Delaney. She had to break glass ceilings for women to become a Cronkite or a Harvey, and she tenaciously did.

In modern times of angle-reporting "news", it would be hard for the old school reporters to keep up with the fantasia of modern newscasting.

Consistently, however, the news has been vacancy regarding the disappearance of Native American women.

The Red Hands symbolizes the ongoing crisis of missing and murdered Indigenous women (MMIW) in the United States, particularly among Native American communities. The red handprint is often seen painted across the mouth of those advocating for the MMIW movement, representing the silenced voices of these women who have been victims of violence, kidnapping, or murder, often without proper investigation or justice.

This crisis is rooted in a long history of systemic marginalization, lack of proper law enforcement response, and jurisdictional challenges.

Red Hands disappearance of Native American women in the United States has been happening for generations. Many Indigenous women go missing or are murdered at rates far higher than other populations, and their cases often go unsolved due to jurisdictional issues between tribal, state, and federal authorities, lack of resources, and societal neglect.

The Red Hands movement has gained traction with advocates, families and activists raising awareness through marches, art, social media campaigns, and legislative efforts. Some states have begun forming task forces to address this, but the issue remains deeply entrenched and complex. The red hands symbolize both the silence imposed on these women and the bloodshed resulting from the violence they face.

The disappearance and murder of Native American women is a tragic and systemic issue.

# Chapter 2

The red hands issue stems from a long history of colonization, violence, and discrimination against Native American communities. Since the arrival of European settlers, indigenous populations have faced genocide, forced relocation, and cultural erasure. Native women, in particular, have been targets of violence, exploitation, and human trafficking. This historical trauma continues to affect Native communities today, manifesting high rates of violence, sexual assault, and kidnapping among Native women.

Native American women are disproportionately affected by violence in that they are 10 times more likely to be murdered compared to other groups of women, and murder is the third leading cause of death for Native women. In addition, Indigenous women face disproportionately high rates of domestic violence and sexual assault. In some regions, Native women disappear at rates that are five to 10 times higher than the national average. In some regions.

Many of these cases go unsolved or uninvestigated due to jurisdictional issues between tribal, state, and federal authorities. Tribal law enforcement is often underfunded and lacks the necessary resources to address the issue, while state or federal authorities may not prioritize these cases or may lack coordination with tribal governments.

The legal complexities around crimes involving Native American women often involve overlapping jurisdictions. Depending on where the crime occurred (on or off a reservation), different agencies may be responsible for investigation and prosecution. This has led to confusion, delays, and in many cases, a lack of accountability.

For example, tribal law enforcement may not have the authority to prosecute non-Native individuals who commit crimes on tribal lands. In addition, federal agencies such as the FBI or the Bureau of Indian Affairs may be responsible for major crimes on reservations, but these cases can be deprioritized or delayed. State law enforcement may not always have the authority to intervene, especially on tribal land.

In recent years, there has been growing awareness and activism around the MMIW crisis, including legislative efforts and grassroots movements such as Savanna's Act. This Act was passed in 2020 and is a federal law aimed at improving data collection and information sharing related to crimes against Native women. It requires the Department of Justice to develop guidelines for responding to cases of missing or murdered Indigenous women and provides more training for law enforcement.

In addition, the Not Invisible Act, which was also passed in 2020, creates a commission made up of law enforcement, tribal leaders, and survivors to address the issue of missing and murdered Indigenous women and human trafficking in Native communities.

Indigenous women, families, and allies have spearheaded the movement for justice through marches, vigils, and art installations.

The red handprint has been a central symbol in these protests, used to raise awareness and amplify the voices of those who have been lost. Annual awareness events, such as the National Day of Awareness for Missing and Murdered Native Women and Murdered Native Women and Girls on May 5th annually have also grown in prominence.

Though different from the United States, Canada has faced a similar crisis, and their Truth and Reconciliation Commission has highlighted the violence against Indigenous women and girls. Many activists in the U.S. draw parallels to the Canadian movement, which includes a National Inquiry into Missing and Murdered Indigenous Women and Girls.

# Chapter 3

The Zodiac Killer is one of the most infamous and mysterious serial killers in American history. Active in northern California during the late 1960s and early 1970s, the killer taunted police and the public with a series of cryptic letters, ciphers, and phone calls. Despite intense investigations, the Zodiac Killer was never caught, and the case remains unsolved to this day.

The Zodiac Killer is confirmed to have murdered at least five people between 1968 and 1969, although he claimed responsibility for as many as 37 victims in his letters. The confirmed attacks targeted young couples, and, in one case, a cab driver.

The Lake Herman Road killing happened on December 20, 1968, and the victims were high school student Betty Lou Jensen, age 16, and her boyfriend, David Faraday, age 17. The young couple were parked on a remote road near Vallejo, California, when the killer approached their car. They were shot and killed with a .22-caliber weapon and this attack was considered the first confirmed Zodiac killing.

The Blue Rock Springs murders happened on July 4, 1969, and the victims were Darlene Ferrin, age 22, and Michael Mageau, age 19. The couple was parked in a car in a similar area near Vallejo when the Zodiac approached, shooting them multiple times with a 9mm handgun. Ferrin died, but Mageau survived despite being critically wounded.

Mageau later gave a description of the killer to the police, describing him as a white man, approximately 5'8", stocky with short light brown hair. This attack was the first to be claimed by the Zodiac Killer in his later ciphers and letters.

The Lake Berryessa murders occurred on September 27, 1969, and the victims were college student Bryan Hartnell, age 20, and his girlfriend, Cecelia Shepard, age 22. The couple was picnicking by Lake Berryessa when the Zodiac approached them wearing a hooded costume with a crosshair symbol on his chest. He tied them up and stabbed them repeatedly. Hartnell survived despite being stabbed six times, but Shepard succumbed to her wounds. The Zodiac later called the police from a payphone to report the crime, taking credit for the attack.

The Presidio Heights murder happened on October 11, 1969, and the victim was Paul Stine, age 29. Paul was a San Francisco taxi driver and was shot in the head while driving in the upscale neighborhood of Presidio Heights. This attack differed from the others in that the victim was not a couple, and the Zodiac didn't use his signature pattern of attacking a couple in a secluded area. Multiple witnesses saw the suspect leaving the scene, and police mistakenly believed the suspect to be African American, allowing the killer to escape.

The Zodiac's letters and ciphers are a major part of his notoriety, and he sent taunting messages to the press and police, claiming credit for the murders and threatening more. Between 1969 and 1974, the Zodiac sent dozens of letters to newspapers like the San Francisco Chronicle, San Francisco Examiner, and Vallejo Times-Herald. These letters were often accompanied by cryptograms, some of which remain unsolved.

# Chapter 4

The first cipher, known as Z408, was sent in July 1969 in a three-part communication to three different newspapers, each containing 408 symbols. This cipher was eventually cracked by a high school teacher and his wife, revealing a message in which the Zodiac bragged about enjoying killing people, comparing it to hunting humans. However, the cipher did not real his identity, as promised.

The next cipher was sent in November 1969 and was a 340-character letter and it remained unsolved for over 50 years until a team of amateur codebreakers cracked it in 2020. The decoded message did not reveal much new information but showed the Zodiac bragging again about his crimes, mocking attempts to catch him, and stating, "I am not afraid of the gas chamber."

The Zodiac frequently signed his letters with a symbol that resembled a crosshair or a gun sight, which became his calling card.

In several letters, the Zodiac threatened to kill more people, including schoolchildren, and he demanded that his letters be printed on the front page of newspapers. He once claimed he had a bomb ready to detonate, but this threat was never carried out.

One letter, known as the "Exorcist letter" in 1974 criticized the movie The Exorcist and contained the chilling phrase, "e – 37, SFPD – 0," implying that he had killed 37 people in the greater San Francisco area without being caught.

# Chapter 5

Despite recent progress in addressing the crisis of missing, kidnapped, or murdered Native American women, many challenges remain at large. One challenge is the gap in accurate data on missing and murdered Indigenous women. Many cases are underreported, and there is no centralized system for tracking these incidents across jurisdictions.

Another issue is the systemic racism against Native Americans, and this often plays a role in the lack of urgency in investigating the disappearance or murder of Native women.

Another issue is human trafficking. Native women and girls are disproportionately vulnerable to human trafficking, especially near oil pipelines or areas where "man camps" have been established for resource extraction industries.

The disappearance and murder of Native American women in the United States is an ongoing tragedy tied to historical and systemic factors that include racism and marginalization of this protected class. Community-led activism has proven to be the most effective tool in raising awareness of this crisis. Indigenous women and their families have long been at the forefront of advocacy efforts to bring attention to the MMIW nightmare.

The National Indigenous Women's Resource Center works to end violence against Native women through education, policy development, and community organization and communication.

The MMIW USA organization provides support to the families of missing and murdered Indigenous women through outreach, education, and communication.

The Violence Against Women Act was reauthorized in 2022 and this bolstered critical provisions for Native American women, expanding the jurisdiction of tribal courts to prosecute non-Native offenders in cases involving domestic violence, sexual assault, and stalking. They helped close a loophole where previously non-Native perpetrators could commit crimes against Native women on tribal lands without facing prosecution due to jurisdictional barriers. This allows tribes to take legal action in ways that they previously couldn't, empowering them to enforce justice within their communities.

Another grassroots effort includes campaigns such as the annual Red Dress Project, where red dresses are hung in public spaces to symbolize the missing women or the MMIW march held every year on May 5th, which is the National Day of Awareness for Missing and Murdered Indigenous Women and Girls.

Public art and symbolism have played a significant role in raising awareness of this tragedy. The red handprint across the face has been used in protests and visual art and has become the symbol for the silenced voices of Indigenous women. In addition, the empty red dresses hung in public places have also become a powerful visual representation of the women who are no longer present in their communities. These dresses evoke a strong, emotional response.

Social media campaigns have also played a key role in amplifying the voices of Native women and their allies.

Hashtags like #MMIW, #MMIWG and #NoMoreStolenSisters have become rallying cries for those seeking justice. These platforms have been crucial in fundraising efforts so that public awareness is increased and there is a social justice fund to fight these crimes.

# Chapter 6

Over the decades, numerous suspects have been proposed as the Zodiac Killer, but none have been definitively linked to the crimes. One of the most prominent suspects was Arthur Leigh Allen. Allen has remained the most widely suspected individual as he was a convicted child molester and was investigated by the police multiple times. Evidence that raised suspicion was the fact that he wore a Zodiac wristwatch with the same crosshair symbol and the fact that he allegedly told a close friend that he fostered a desire to kill couples. In addition, he lived near the locations of the Zodiac killings. His handwriting was similar, but there was no conclusive match. He was exonerated as a suspect when his fingerprints and DNA did not match those found on the Zodiac's letters.

Lawrence Kane was a convicted felon and had been linked to several disappearances in the 1960s. A retired police officer claimed that Kane matched a description provided by one of the Zodiac victims who survived the attack. However, there was no definitive proof linking him to the murders.

Richard Gaikowski was formerly a journalist and filmmaker and became a suspect due to his erratic behavior and connections to the Bay Area. Some claim that his voice matched that of the voice on the payphone when the Zodiac called to report a murder, but no concrete evidence regarding this claim ever came to fruition.

Ted Kaczynski, the Unabomber, was also a suspect as well as Bruce Davis who was a member of the Manson murderers, but neither could be solidly linked to the Zodiac murders.

# Chapter 7

The Zodiac investigation involved various police departments and the FBI, who gathered fingerprints, handwriting samples, and even DNA from a stamp on one of the letters. However, none of this evidence matched anyone identifiable in CODIS, the storage locker for criminal evidence and DNA matching.

It is fair to say that the Zodiac Killer has remained a legend in the world of unsolved crime, to the extent that it carries a sort of pulp fiction in pop culture, inspiring movies, TV shows, books, and series.

There are many movies made about these crimes including "Zodiac" from 2007 directed by David Fincher, "Dirty Harry" made in 1971 starring Clint Eastwood as "Scorpio", and numerous others.

The Zodiac Killer case is unique in its combination of unsolved murders, cryptic ciphers, and public taunts. It remains unknown if she really killed 37 people as it seemed like an exaggeration of a man with delusions of grandeur.

It would seem in this day of AI and advancements in DNA that something would have matched by now. For example, recently updated evidence was used to finally catch the Golden State Killer. After that discovery, it was presumed that DNA would link someone to the Zodiac Killer, but this has yet to happen and this serial killer case remains unsolved.

# Chapter 8

There exists a lack of comprehensive data on missing and murdered Indigenous women. Many cases go unreported or are not properly documented as there isn't an organized database for all reporting. According to the Urban Indian Health Institute, police departments often misclassify or undercount these types of cases. Data collection needs to improve across all jurisdictions, including federal, state, and tribal so that the full scope of this crisis can be addressed globally.

One primary obstacle to justice for Native women is the complex web of jurisdictional authority on tribal lands. It is a mixed bag in that the Native tribes enjoy their jurisdictional authority over their tribes and their land, but the flip side of this equation is that usurps federal and state authority to prosecute crime on tribal land, and thus, underreporting, and undercharging cases.

Crimes committed on tribal lands might involve tribal law enforcement, state police, and federal agencies, depending on the nature of the crime and the identity of the perpetrator. Historically, these agencies have not coordinated effectively, leading the delayed or incomplete investigations.

The recent expansion of tribal jurisdiction, especially under the Violence Against Women Act, helps address this issue, but enforcement and resources for tribal courts and police forces remain limited.

In addition to this, systemic racism and discrimination continue to play a role in the MMIW crisis.

Indigenous women often face indifference from law enforcement, resulting in slower investigations and lower prioritization of their cases. Family members and advocates frequently report dismissive attitudes from police and delays in filing missing person reports.

Many Indigenous women live in poverty or face social marginalization, making them more vulnerable to violence, trafficking, and exploitation. In regions where industries like oil extraction bring an influx of transient workers such as the "man camps", Native women are particularly susceptible to human trafficking and violence. These comps are often linked to increased crime, and local law enforcement may not have the resources to deal with the resulting issues.

# Chapter 9

There remains a growing concern that the Zodiac Killer is part of a broader network of serial killers that prey on vulnerable populations, such as Indigenous women. The Zodiac's penchant for cryptic communication and taunting law enforcement could have a link to the Red Hand missing or murdered Indigenous women.

The FBI, during a recent investigation into the murder of a Crow Native American woman, found a cipher left at the murder scene. The cipher was a drawing on the victim's inner thigh of a zodiac symbol that resembled a crosshair or a gun sight, as a signature to the murder. This cipher or symbol resembled the Zodiac Killer's motive operandi, and this raised severe concern with law enforcement and Native Americans alike.

This "calling card" is not the first time that this has happened in the Red Hand murders. In fact, several of the most recent victims had this "calling card" drawn on their inner thigh. This particular murder of the Crow Native woman happened in Sheridan County, Wyoming, near a small town called Wyarno. Wyarno is an unincorporated community in central Sheridan County and lies along Wyoming Highway 336, approximately 10 miles east of Sheridan. Although Wyarno is unincorporated, it has a post office with a ZIP code of its own. This Crow Native grew up there. It is not far from the Crow reservation that exists in southern Montana where she was born.

When Mary MacIntosh was informed of the murder that took place within her jurisdiction, she knew that she needed to take swift action.

These missing and murdered Indigenous women were a huge concern to people in the area, and the abductions and murders were happening at an alarmingly frequent pace. There had been few prosecutions of these crimes, and this was intolerable, especially on her watch.

Mac immediately called her husband, Burg, who was the Sheriff in town. As the prosecuting attorney in Sheridan County, Mac had to seek swift justice, and Burg would be more than willing to help her. They spoke on the phone about this victim and the "calling card" left behind. Once Mac hung up, she requested that her paralegal roll up her sleeves and get to work on identifying the "calling card" of the crosshair or gun sight and see what this clue could represent.

When her paralegal informed her that it resembled the cipher of the Zodiac Killer, she was alarmed. If this was the work of the Zodiac Killer or a copycat serial killer, the community at large was at risk.

# Chapter 10

Mac was on the phone with an FBI agent who was assigned to investigate this most recent murder, and this man had also been involved in the ongoing Zodiac Killer investigations early in his career as an agent. He knew nearly every detail of the Zodiac murders and the clues and ciphers left behind, and the recent murders of the Native women with the "calling card" drawn on their inner thigh were highly concerning to him. If this was the Zodiac or a copycat of the Zodiac, he knew that there was a large community of women at risk.

If these last few murders of Native American women in northern Wyoming and southern Montana were part of a pattern of ritualistic killing that is continuing today as copycat Zodiac murders, then the Red Hand murders that have been ongoing for decades could be terrifying. If there was a tie between the hundreds of Red Hand murders of Native women in the United States and the Zodiac Killer, then this serial killer's motive made some sense. It frightened Mac, and it was gravely concerning to the FBI agent.

The FBI did not officially handle the Zodiac Killer case early on, as it was primarily under the jurisdiction of local law enforcement agencies such as the San Francisco Police Department. However, the FBI became involved over time, and a notable FBI criminal profiler and a notable young agent were assigned to the case. John E. Douglas was a pioneer young FBI agent introducing what would come to be commonly referred to as a criminal profiler.

Douglas became famous for his work in criminal psychology and is one of the inspirations for the character Holden Ford in the popular TV show, Mindhunter.

Douglas joined the FBI in the early 1970s and became one of the first criminal profilers. Though not a central figure at the very start of the Zodiac case, his work in the Behavioral Science Unit helped advance the understanding of serial killers, including the Zodiac. He later provided insight into the Zodiac's psychological profile.

Douglas was recently retired from the FBI, but when a few of the Red Hand murders had ciphers or "calling cards" etched onto their inner thighs, he was called back to duty to investigate.

He promptly made an appointment to meet with Mac and Burg to discuss the most recent killing in Sheridan County, Wyoming.

# Chapter 11

Mac received a telephone call from The Sheridan Press, a local newspaper in Sheridan. The editor told Mac that she just received in the mail a letter regarding the most recent Red Hand murder, and it seemed to be a cipher or code that the editorial team could not decipher. It was an encryption that was unreadable.

Mac asked that they send her a copy via email so that she could share it with FBI agent John E. Douglas. The FBI criminal profiler team could put the cipher into their algorithm to try to decode it. The FBI uses what is known as AES which stands for Advanced Encryption Standard to decode ciphers.

Mac had a meeting set for later that afternoon with John Douglas, who was en route from headquarters located at the J. Edgar Hoover Building located at 935 Pennsylvania Avenue NW in Washington, D.C. Once she received the email from the Sheridan Press, she forwarded it to John E. Douglas with a note that explained how she had come into possession of the cipher and what she and the editor of the newspaper thought that it represented.

In the meantime, Mac needed a press conference, and she had a call with CBS Correspondent Kate Donnelly, who Mac had met during the investigation of Deputy Dawg/DB Cooper's investigation of the murder of the then sheriff in Sheridan. Kate Donnelly was new in the investigatory journalism world at the time, and she was named after the GOAT Kate Delany, the woman who broke glass ceilings for women as sports broadcasters in sports.

Mac needed to get ahead of this story. A copycat serial killer who just killed a Native American woman in her jurisdiction. She needed to learn everything about the Red Hand missing and murdered women in the United States, and she needed to learn everything about the Zodiac Killer and his crimes and ciphers, and she needed a one-hour crash course with Kate Donnelly before the press conference that Kate had called.

The learning curve would be high. The hours would be long.

And Mac was a new mother of twin boys, and she was going to be away from home a lot.

Her husband, Burg, the Sheriff in town, was still on paternity leave and taking care of their boys with aplomb. He was actually grateful that his wife was too busy to be home because he was never home when his girls from his previous marriage were little, so he always felt fatherhood guilt. Now, as much as he didn't want Mac to feel that same guilt, he was able to satiate his own guilt by being a stay-at-home dad on paternity leave and taking care of their newborns.

# Chapter 12

The Zodiac Killer gave himself the name "Zodiac" in one of the many letters he sent to the press. However, the term "Zodiac" was never directly linked to any personal or astrological significance by the killer, adding to the mystery.

The Zodiac sent several cryptic letters, with some ciphers still unsolved. The most famous cipher, Z340, remained unsolved for 51 years until a team of codebreakers deciphered it in 2020, though it didn't reveal the killer's identity. Some of his other messages, like Z13 and Z32 ciphers, remain unsolved.

Some investigators believe the Zodiac may have had a military background, based on the precision of his codes and cryptograms, as well as his knowledge of firearms.

In many of his letters, Zodiac stated that his murder was collecting "slaves" for the afterlife. This bizarre motive has sparked theories connecting him to various fringe belief systems or psychological conditions.

A boot print, specifically a Wing Walker military-style boot, was found at the crime scene of one of the Zodiac's attacks at Lake Berryessa near Napa, California. These boots were commonly worn by military personnel, fueling speculation about the killer's background.

Despite claims of being responsible for 37 murders, only five confirmed killings are attributed to the Zodiac. However, some believe the Zodiac's murders might extend to other states, like Nevada, Wyoming, Montana, or the Dakotas. Perhaps, as far as Oklahoma.

Zodiac was notorious for taunting the police and press with letters, sometimes containing pieces of his victims' clothing as proof. E once even called the police himself after committing a murder in the Vallejo area of California. He called to "report the crime" and then to brag about it.

The Zodiac often claimed that one of his victims survived. Kathleen Johns, who was abducted but managed to escape in 1970, believed her captor was the Zodiac, though this has never been confirmed.

The Zodiac's signature crosshair symbol has never been definitively explained, but some think it could be based on a gun sight or a reference to astrological symbols. It also appeared on watch brands called "Zodiac."

Over the years, numerous amateur sleuths and investigators have proposed a wide range of suspects, from Ted Kaczynski (the Unabomber) to even well-known individuals. Some people have even theorized that the Zodiac may have known one of the victims personally. Some believe he was a retired police officer.

Despite the multitude of clues, ciphers, cryptograms, and taunts, the Zodiac Killer's identity has remained elusive.

# Chapter 13

The phenomenon of missing and murdered Indigenous women is a deeply troubling issue in North America. The red handprint, often painted across the mouth in protests and art, symbolizes the silence and erasure of Indigenous women who have been abducted, murdered, or gone missing. This powerful symbol represents the voice of violence, and the red color is often associated with both life and blood in many Indigenous cultures, signifying both vitality and the violence that has been inflicted.

Many missing Indigenous women are linked to human trafficking. Native American missing women are disproportionately affected by human trafficking due to their marginalization, geographic isolation, and lack of protection from law enforcement. Major highways like the "Highway of Tears" in British Columbia have become notorious routes where many Indigenous women have disappeared.

One major factor in the crisis is the complex jurisdictional tangle between federal, state, and tribal authorities, and crimes committed on tribal land can fall under different legal jurisdictions, depending on factors like the ethnicity of the perpetrator or victim, leading to confusion and delayed responses from law enforcement.

Indigenous women's disappearances and murders often receive little to no media attention compared to cases involving white women, a phenomenon known as "missing white woman syndrome." This lack of coverage further contributes to the invisibility of the issue.

The violence against Indigenous women is deeply rooted in colonialism. Historical trauma, displacement, and the systemic destruction of Indigenous communities and cultures have created conditions in which Native women are more vulnerable to violence. Residential schools, forced relocations, and the breaking of treaties have all contributed to this crisis.

Temporary work camps set up near Indigenous lands for oil, gas, or mining projects, known as "man camps," have been linked to spikes in violence against Native women. The influx of predominantly male workers into these remote areas has been associated with increased rates of sexual violence, harassment, and human trafficking.

Indigenous women have been at the forefront of the movement to address this crisis. Groups like the Native Women's Association of Canada and Sisters in Spirit, as well as individual activists, have been critical in raising awareness and pushing for justice. Their grassroots efforts have been instrumental in making this issue more visible to the public and policymakers.

Art plays a powerful role in the movement, with many artists using red hand imagery, beadwork, and other traditional forms to honor the missing women. The REDress Project, an art installation by Metis artist Jaime Black, features empty red dresses hanging in public spaces to represent the missing and murdered women and has become an internationally recognized symbol.

In response to growing awareness, some legal reforms have been enacted, such as the passage of Savanna's Act in the U.S. in 2020.

31

Named after Savanna LaFontaine-Greywind, a 22-year-old Indigenous woman who was murdered in 2017, the act aims to improve data collection and coordination among law enforcement agencies to address the crisis of missing and murdered Indigenous women.

The Red Hand and the MMIW crisis shed light on a profound issue of violence and neglect that Native communities face, and the ongoing efforts to raise awareness and secure justice for these women are central to the movement.

# Chapter 14

There have been cases involving the identification of Native American murder victims using forensic dentistry, though it is often hard to pinpoint specific cases where the "Red Hands" has been involved without more details. Dr. Michelle Meehan and Dr. Kate Meehan Murphy are local Sheridan, Wyoming forensic dentists who together are a team who have been involved in such a task force to identify. Forensics, particularly dental records, have been crucial in identifying badly decayed remains. In many MMIWG cases, remains have been so decomposed that traditional identification methods are ineffective, leaving dental and DNA analysis as the primary tools.

A well-known case involving forensic dental identification of a Native American victim was that of Wilma Mankiller, though she wasn't connected to the Red Hand or MMIWG. Additionally, several MMIWG cases have used forensic dentistry for identification, but individual names of victims in decayed conditions may not always be made public out of respect for privacy and the families. However, some of the well-known Native American women who have tragically become victims of murder, and whose cases are part of the broader MMIWG crisis include Savanna LaFontaine-Greywind, who was a member of the Spirit Lak Nation in North Dakota.

Savanna was murdered in 2017 while eight months pregnant, which drew national attention to the epidemic of violence against Indigenous women.

Hanna Harris, who was a member of the Northern Cheyenne tribe in Montana, was murdered in 2013 and her body was found days later. Her death prompted the creation of Hanna's Act in Montana to improve investigation processes for missing Indigenous people.

Ashley Loring Heavy Runner, who was a member of the Blackfeet Nation in Montana, disappeared in 2017, and her case remains unsolved. She has become a symbol for many missing Indigenous women whose cases receive little attention.

Olivia Lone Bear, who was a member of Three Affiliated Tribes in North Dakota, went missing in 2017, and her body was found months later in her submerged truck. The circumstances surrounding her death are still unclear.

Kaysera Stops Pretty Places was a member of the Crow and Northern Cheyenne tribes in Montana, in 2019, Kaysera was found dead under suspicious circumstances, and her family continues to advocate for justice.

While the term "Red Hand" is used symbolically for the MMIWG movement, there isn't a specific group or individual perpetrator known as "Red Hand" responsible for these deaths. The red handprint across the mouth is a visual seen in many protests and it symbolizes the silencing of Native women and girls through violence and societal neglect. The movement encompasses thousands of cases, many of which remain unsolved or under-reported.

The new development of the "calling card" of the crosshair insignia on the inner thigh of recent Indigenous murder victims has raised awareness in this region, and Mary MacIntosh was determined to get to the bottom of the case that was on her desk. She was anxiously awaiting the arrival of the FBI agent later that day.

# Chapter 15

Mac was delighted that FBI special agent John E. Douglas was willing to fly from Washington, D.C. to Sheridan, Wyoming to meet with her regarding the case of the murder victim found nearby in Wyarno. The victim was identified forensically by Drs. Michelle Meehan and Kate Meehan Murphy via dental records were positively identified as Tammy RunsLikeDoe.

Douglas poured over the file as an expert criminal profiler, and he made notes on his legal notepad. He was meticulous with detail and did not speak with Mac until he had read and devoured every last word.

"I've seen facts like this before," Douglas said to Mac in a very even and succinct manner. "This is going to sound a little far-fetched, but I believe this to be the work of an underground shadowy crew that targets Indigenous women in the United States and leaves behind these ciphers to taunt law enforcement, much like the Zodiac Killer did in the 1960s and 1970s."

"What other cases have you seen with facts that mirror this one?" Mac asked.

"We have an open case here in Wyoming over by Devils Tower where a Native woman was killed in much the same way," Douglas said.

"Why have I not heard of it?" Mac asked. "I hear of all murders in Wyoming. There aren't many of them."

"Because Native American women murders are seriously under-reported in the United States. It is savage to think that such an important culture is so marginalized and discriminated against. It has bothered me for decades," Douglas said emphatically. "Law enforcement doesn't seem to take these Red Hand cases seriously."

"Why? That seems absolutely ludicrous," Mac said.

"That's an understatement, but it is true," Douglas continued. "The Devils Tower case was on sacred ground, as if taunting the cops wasn't enough. It was also taunting the family and the Indigenous people as a whole."

"I invited a journalist from New York to Sheridan to cover this case. Would you mind if I invited her to my office so that she could pick your brain regarding these Red Hand killings and the associated ciphers?" Mac asked. "I feel like these victims deserve national media attention, which they clearly are not getting, and it is what I call social injustice."

"I welcome it," Douglas replied.

Mac picked up her cell phone and quickly texted Kate Donnelly an invite.

"I just sent her a note, so hopefully she is nearby and can pop over. She's staying downtown at the Historic Sheridan Inn," Mac said.

"That's where I am staying as well," Douglas said. "It is a beautiful hotel and the history surrounding it is incredible. Buffalo Bill Cody. Ernest Hemingway. I could continue. I was reading about it on the plane," Douglas said.

"Yes, it is a treasure in Sheridan, for sure," Mac said.

It wasn't long before there was a knock on Mac's conference room door. It was Kate Donnelly.

# Chapter 16

Mac quickly introduced Kate to John Douglas and they exchanged brief niceties before rolling up their sleeves and getting to work on the facts of the case of Tammy RunsLikeDoe and the other Red Hand murders in the United States. Kate was well-versed in the Red Hand killings as a news reporter, and she was well aware of who John E. Douglas was. Kate was invigorated to be in his presence as he was known to be the best criminal profiler that the FBI had.

John Douglas continued to bring Kate up to speed. "This shadowy criminal network or cult-like underground organization is known as The Blood Cresent. It is a secretive group that operates within the depths of hell, and it is known for trafficking Native American women while cloaking its true objectives in occultism and cryptic rituals," he explained. "The Blood Cresent originated from an ancient secret society, a splinter group of the Freemasons, that merged dark rituals with colonial ambitions during the westward expansion. They exploit sacred Native American burial grounds and legends, believing that through sacrificial blood rituals, they can access hidden powers or supernatural protection."

Kate and Mac were both taking copious notes during this monologue.

"Go on," Mac urged. Kate nodded her head in agreement. Mac's conference room seemed to shrink a little and the lighting felt like it had dimmed.

"Their ideology revolves around a twisted interpretation of the cycles of nature, believing that harvesting the blood of those connected to the land, such as Native land, could ultimately align their organization with mystical control over Mother Earth and hidden knowledge," Douglas explained.

"How dark is this group?" Kate asked.

"Dark. This group poses as various charitable organizations, philanthropic clubs, or land developers in reservation areas. They secretly engage in trafficking, taking advantage of the high rates of missing Native American women, whom they abduct for their sacrificial rites.

"How could they possibly think or behave this way? Are they cavemen?" Mac asked incredulously.

"Sort of," John agreed. "Using coded communication through symbolic ciphers, they carry out their operations without being detected by the authorities. These ciphers often incorporate Native American symbolism, Freemason symbols, and coded references to celestial events."

"If the FBI knows so much about The Blood Cresent group, then why haven't you caught them? Kate astutely asked.

"Believe me, we are trying!" John said emphatically.

"You have to know who some of them are," Mac stated.

"Not really. They operate in plain site with everyday jobs that are legal. And it's not illegal to join a social group such as the Masons or the Eagles or any other number of groups that exist legally in society."

"If you don't mind," Mac interrupted, "I'm going to call my husband, Burg, who is the town sheriff, to come down to hear the rest of this story.

He'll need to hear it in person to believe it. I'll have my staff order us dinner delivered here at my office and we can continue this over a working meal," Mac suggested.

# Chapter 17

Mac brought Burg up to speed over dinner before they would continue the conversation with John Douglas.

"The group's symbolic language is key to their operations," John resumed. "The 'Red Hand' is a marker left at the scene of each killing, often smeared in blood, representing both the violent act and their connection to an ancient handprint symbol associated with power over life and death. Each handprint is accompanied by cryptic, hand-carved ciphers in surrounding rocks or walls – symbols only understood by the high-ranking members of the cult or group."

"These ciphers, are they anything similar to the Zodiac Killer ciphers and the one that was received by The Sheridan Press?" Mac asked.

"Yes. These ciphers could be made up of hybrid glyphs that mix Native American petroglyphs with astrological symbols and Freemason codes. These symbols might provide clues to law enforcement if they can break the code, revealing hidden locations of bodies or planned future abductions," John replied.

"What did you say the name of this underground group is?" Burg asked.

"The Blood Cresent," Kate replied.

"Yes," John continued, "The Blood Cresent performs ritualistic killings in line with lunar cycles, believing that their dark rites are most powerful under the crescent moon.

These killings are not random; each victim is part of a pre-determined list that ensures the completion of a greater occult ritual meant to awaken what they believe is an ancient, hidden power buried within the sacred tribal lands."

"The next crescent moon should be sometime next week," Mac said. "Should we be concerned?"

"Yes, you should be alarmed by this, as the autopsy report on Tammy RunsLikeDoe showed that she was killed at or near a crescent moon cycle," John explained.

"We better be on high alert," Burg suggested.

"Yes, you'd better," John agreed.

# Chapter 18

When Mac and Burg got home, it was late, and Burg's mother was asleep on the couch with her reading glasses still on and a book sprawled on her chest. The twins were asleep in their cribs. They tiptoed upstairs to tuck the baby boys in and make sure that the nightlight was on and the baby monitor was working. All was well.

Burg's mother had decided to move from Cheyenne to Sheridan to help the nanny with the twins. They were her only grandsons, as Burg's daughters were grown and on their own. It was a Godsend to have her living with them, as their schedules were unpredictable. Burg could get called in anytime, and Mac was known to get to the office early and leave late, especially if she was in the middle of a trial.

Mac and Burg were exhausted but also invigorated by John Douglas and his wealth and breadth of information as an FBI profiler. He was so very articulate and knew these types of cases like the back of his hand. He could explain the ciphers and their meanings all night long. He was fascinating, but the facts were terrifying. The murder of Tammy RunsLikeDoe had folk around Sheridan petrified about the next murder.

The Red Hands crisis was very real in the western states, particularly in North and South Dakota, Montana, and Wyoming. The MMIW movement was gaining traction in these states, and people, particularly Native Americans, were fearful for their lives and the lives of their loved ones.

Indigenous women were being abducted or murdered at an increasingly higher rate, and it seemed like there was no rhyme or reason for when they happened. Some happened in the middle of the day and others occurred at night.

Weekdays and weekends were not distinguishable from these crimes, making it very difficult to predict or prepare for.

Burg had the funny feeling in his stomach that the next week was not going to be good. Mac shared the same feeling. And to make matters worse, there was no suspect for the murder of Tammy RunsLikeDoe, and other than the cipher sent to The Sheridan Press and the insignia left on the inner thigh of the victim, there were no leads that tied this murder to any suspect.

# Chapter 19

The next day, John Douglas and Kate Donnelly returned to Mac's office to continue going through evidence and to discuss John's profiling theories.

"The Blood Cresent group has an ultimate goal to secure dominance over significant spiritual sites such as the Medicine Wheel found in your local Bighorn Mountains, and Devils Tower located in the easter part of Wyoming. Their goal is to use these sites to channel powers they believe will grant them immortality or godlike control over the region," John stated.

"That sounds pretty out there," Kate said.

"It is out there. They are far-fetched folks. We at the FBI think that by nature these members are loners and that they join this sort of a cult in order to fit in It's the only thing that makes sense to us at the Bureau."

"That is the only thing that makes sense to me, too," Mac agreed.

"Now let's put two concepts together. At the FBI, we have come to the conclusion that The Red Hand Killers are an elite sect within The Blood Crescent, serving as the enforcers and executioners of the organization's will. They are notorious for leaving their signature red handprint at the scene of abductions and murders," John suggested.

"This concept makes the Freemasons look tame," Kate said.

"Yes. It should alarm you."

"It alarms Burg and me quite a bit," Mac said. "We were up half the night worried about it. It was almost a blessing to do the midnight feeding of our twins!"

"Continue to consider that each member of the Red Hand Killers is bound by a blood oath, sworn in the secret, brutal initiation ceremony. They are known to communicate using an obscure cipher that weaves symbolism from Native American creation myths with hidden messages encoded using methods like the Vigenere cipher, visible only under certain conditions like moonlight or using specific chemical reactions," John said.

That caught the attention of Kate and Mac.

# Chapter 20

John continued to educate Kate and Mac over lunch downtown.

"Not many people know this, but in the 1970s, we believed that the Zodiac Killer was a retired San Francisco police officer because he had to have known where to find specific victims and how not to get caught for murder."

"Did you ever suspect any one person over another?" Kate asked.

"Not really. Not specifically, but I did have my eye on a guy that had recently retired, but I was a very young agent at the time, and I was tentative to speak up," John admitted.

"Did you think it would backfire on you and cause you to be reassigned or something along those lines?" Mac asked.

"Yes. Very much. But to this day, I strongly believe that the Zodiac was a retired copy. I also believe that this cultish network of The Red Hand Killers and/or The Blood Crescent people could have corrupt individuals within law enforcement or even government agencies, covering up the disappearances of Native women or redirecting investigations. It would make sense that they would maintain power by blackmailing officials or luring them into their secret cult with promises of influence and wealth," John suggested.

"That would freak Burg out, big time," Mac said.

"It freaks some of us out at the Bureau. It implies that it is going to be very difficult to crack the case if insiders are scrambling the clues," John said.

# Chapter 21

When we catch this killer, what expert witnesses will I need to prove my murder in the first degree case? Mac asked John Douglas. She was always mentally preparing for trial, and she was convinced that they would catch the perpetrator the following week during the crescent moon.

"You will need a Native American cultural expert and tribal elder who understands the ancient symbols for testimony, but it might be hard to ascertain this person to testify because most of these people are petrified with fear regarding retaliation for revealing the dark truth about the Blood Crescent," John replied flatly. He understood that this was a frustrating answer to give to a woman who had never lost a trial in her career.

"Don't the tribal elders want the Red Hand killings to stop?" Mac asked incredulously. She was mystified by his answer.

"Of course they do, but keep in mind that they have been running scared for centuries. Natives were run off their lands and forced onto reservations and have lost their freedoms and rights. They have been lied to and deceived since colonial days, and they don't inherently trust white people."

"Describe to me what you envision one of these murders to look like. Who are we looking for?" Mac asked.

"As a profiler, I believe that we are hunting a white man or a group of white men who systematically hate Native women. These guys could be woman haters in general and add to it a deep sense of discrimination against Indigenous people as a whole.

I believe they are cultists, and they enjoy the only comradery that they have in their lives. The comradery of a cult membership with a commonality of hate," John said.

"Keep going," Mac urged.

"I think that the Red Hand killer or killers could include someone with a deep understanding of both the Zodiac's methods and Native American history, blending the two into a complex web of cryptic killings. This person or persons could be a former student of the Zodiac case, possibly even a relative of a survivor or victim from his original killing spree," John said.

"Would family members of the Zodiac's original victims or survivors who have been haunted by the unsolved case be possible suspects in the Red Hand murders?" Mac asked.

"Excellent question," John said. "We profilers at the FBI have always believed that the copycat serial killers involved in the Red Hand killings are highly likely to be relatives of either the Zodiac himself or the survivors of the Zodiac. We believe that the obsession would need to run deep,"

"That makes sense to me, and to Burg. We have spoken of it at length, and Burg has a true knack for forensic criminal analysis," Mac said.

"One has to conclude that the weaving of the Zodiac Killer with the Red Hand killings or Native American women must amalgamate the elements of deeper social issues, all while maintaining the tension and psychological intrigue typical with someone or somebodies with such an obsession," John explained.

"Again, that makes sense," Mac agreed.

"What happens if we never find the Red Hand killer or killers?" Mac asked. "What if this turns out to be like the Zodiac case and there is no closure and the body count will simply increase at a rapid pace?"

"It is highly possible, maybe probable, knowing how long this has been going on without a trace of evidence that points in any one direction," John admitted.

"You know that I have never lost a case, right?" Mac asked.

"I am aware of your track record."

"I am not okay with not finding the perpetrator of this murder."

"I would hope not for a number of reasons," John said bluntly.

"We are going to find this person or this group, and we are going to prosecute them to the fullest extent possible," Mac said with conviction.

John nodded, without the same level of confidence.

# Chapter 22

The Blood Crescent originated from an ancient secret society, a splinter group of the Freemasons that merged dark rituals with colonial ambitions during the westward expansion. They exploit sacred Native American burial grounds and legends, believing that through sacrificial blood rituals, they can access hidden powers or supernatural protection. Their ideology revolves around a twisted interpretation of the cycles of nature, believing that harvesting the blood of those connected to the Native land and mystical control over the earth and hidden knowledge.

The waxing and waning moon symbolizes the transition between life and death. The night of the crescent moon is considered a spiritual turning point in the culture of Native Americans. There exists a belief that souls can more easily transition between worlds during this phase, making it a night for rituals involving death or rebirth.

Native Americans believe that the crescent moon is a time of increased vulnerability, particularly for women. This belief stems from ancient folklore.

In addition, The Freemasons believe that the crescent moon and its lunar power are symbolic of vulnerability.

The crescent moon dates back to colonial history and appropriation. It links Native American women's heritage and identity, representing her connection to her ancestors. A Red Blood killer chooses this night out of hatred or greed to strike, believing that by doing so, they sever that connection, thus gaining some form of power or control.

This is loosely translated into historical conflicts where sacred symbols and times are disrespected by colonial forces.

The crescent moon and the death of a Native woman mark a cosmic alignment where nature seems to bear witness to human actions. There is a sense of foreboding like Mac and Burg were experiencing.

# Chapter 23

Many Native women link the crescent moon with the revelation of hidden truths and when the physical and spiritual worlds blur.

The crescent moon symbolizes a time when the boundary between life and death is thin, similar to the concept of Samhain or Dia de los Muertos in other cultures.

# Chapter 24

Mac and Burg were on edge. The crescent moon was two days away and their household felt strained. Even the twins felt it. They were fussy and they normally were not.

Mac felt so disconnected because there was no suspect and she also felt frustrated. She needed to nest with her babies and cook and clean and she took a few days off.

She and Burg invited both Kate and John to stay with them. They readily accepted. In this six-bedroom house, they could create their own "war room" to discuss these murders but remain out of the public eye, and it gave Mac the time she needed with her newborn babies.

Burg was delighted. He had growing concerns that her immersion into work was a sign of rejection.

Her redesign of the working relationship gave him the peace that he needed.

He had always felt that he married up with Mac. She had never been married, and she was smarter, younger, more fit, and more financially secure. None of these things ever crossed Mac's mind. She married Burg without question, and she was entirely unconcerned about the things he never told her because she was unaware of them.

Her love was pure and true.

# Chapter 25

The crescent moon symbolizes a time when boundary between life and death.

Mac was closely tied to the Red Hands movement as her best friend growing up was a Crow Native American. She attended marches with a red handprint across her mouth and she donated to the legal defense fund for Red Hand victims.

It is Native belief that women and elders are particularly vulnerable under a crescent moon. This belief is based on an old superstition and longstanding belief tied to lunar cycles.

Mac and Burg had a growing concern that the Red Hands killer knew of the superstition and was using it in a manipulative manner during the upcoming lunar phase, believing that the next victim would be easier to control or harm.

# Chapter 26

Chastidy GrizzlyBear was a precocious teenager and at age 17, she defied her parents regularly. The entire Sheridan County was on lockdown by order of the sheriff, as it was a crescent moon and the community at large was terrified that a Red Hand killer was on the prowl.

The town was on edge. Even the Mint Bar, the Rainbow Bar, and the Last Chance Bar were closed for the night, which never happened. The sheriff ordered it to protect the citizens and there was a curfew from eight in the evening until six in the morning, unless one had a job that required work during these hours. Burg would not have more blood on his hands if he could avoid it. Mac supported this wholeheartedly.

"Do you think that a curfew and a lockdown of this town will keep the Red Hands killer from killing?" John Douglas asked Mac earlier that day.

"I don't know, John, but we can't just sit around and do nothing and wait for our next victim to show up. I am losing sleep over this. I have participated in Red Hands demonstrations for decades and I am sick to death over these murders. It is cold blood murder, and it seems to be foreseeable and preventable."

Mac was passionate about this cause. It was transparently clear.

"Murderers like this type of guardedness, Mary. They love the paranoia, and they feed on it. They like the fact that they have an entire community backed into a corner. They are bullies. This is their cup of tea.

I wish I could have talked you and Burg out of this curfew concept. I think it will backfire," John said plainly.

"Burg and I are not the 'wait and see' types."

"Red Hand Killers are."

"John, I respect you at a very high level and I am grateful for your help on this case. We are likely not going to agree on everything, but we are here to work together as a team, and there is substantial value in that," Mac said.

"Agreed."

# Chapter 27

Chastidy GrizzlyBear was defiant of rules, and the imposed curfew was a mere hurdle to her. A challenge.

She snuck out of her house in Dayton, Wyoming around nine in the evening, after dark, and she intended to meet her boyfriend at the Parkman Bar parking lot. The bar was closed as a result of the curfew, and it was walking distance from her house. Her boyfriend was older, age 20, and drove a pickup truck.

Chastidy never made it to the Parkman Bar parking lot.

# Chapter 28

Word got out quickly of her death. Chastidy was found in the Dayton town park, partly disrobed, with a crosshair imprinted on her inner thigh and her own bloody handprint across her mouth.

When Burg got the call in the early hours of the morning, his spirit shrank. When he told Mac, she responded per her norm. She was pissed. She was angry that this happened again to a Native woman, and she was angry that the perpetrator was still on the loose, but she hated most was the pain and suffering that her family and friends were enduring.

John Douglas was waiting in the conference room when Mac arrived at her office. She had stopped by Java Moon Café downtown and bought them both coffee and a slice of their delicious lemon cake, and handed him both before they spoke.

"I know what you are going to say, and I am not prepared emotionally to deal with it," Mac professed.

"We need to look at this together square in the face. You need to hold a press conference with Kate this morning, and the community needs answers. If you don't, this will spin out of control quickly," John told her.

"You are probably correct. My stomach hurts. My heart hurts. I could not let go of my twins this morning, and I hated leaving them, despite knowing that they are safe in my home."

"Understandable. I feel your pain. I've been doing this a long, long time, and I know that communities fray if you don't stay ahead of the communication with your constituents," John recommended.

"Let's call Kate and have her set up a press conference and let's brainstorm our questions to feed to her that we are prepared to answer."

"Okay, I will call her now, but I think I should begin the press conference by introducing you and allowing you to field the grounders on this one. I'm too emotionally fragile, and quite frankly, you are better versed in this," Mac said.

"I don't disagree, but your face has to be the first that this community sees. They trust you. I think Burg needs to be standing either at your side or immediately to your right so that the community sees the unity of force with law enforcement," John suggested.

"I will call him now," Mac said.

# Chapter 29

There existed a clash between modern law enforcement and ancient, mystical traditions. The symbolism of the crescent moon ties into themes of secrecy, as the crescent reveals only part of the whole truth, which was reelected on Mac's investigation into the Freemasons and the Blood Crescent secret society.

The crescent moon is a symbol of the Native American woman's cultural identity. Mac and John spoke before the press conference of the concept that the killer or killers might be seeking to erase the Native woman's heritage, either through an act of hate or to exploit something sacred to her people, such as land, artifacts, or spiritual knowledge.

"I am very worried about what could happen next month in June," Mac stated.

"What is so special about June?" John asked.

"The Medicine Wheel is closed to the public for the month of June, as Native American tribes from all over this country meet there for cultural worship and ceremonies. I'm worried that the Red Hand killer will be lying in wait, seeking out that lone wolf Native woman to kill at the Medicine Wheel. That would be a strong, vile message to Natives," Mac suggested.

John Douglas nodded. He was not as versed as Mac in Native culture, but she had a valid point.

"If the killer strikes during this religious time for Natives, he or she could be knowingly sending a message or making a point – either to disrupt the cultural practice of Natives at the Medicine Wheel or to gain power or control over the Native land or people," Mac said.

"Do we include this in the press conference?" John asked.

"I don't know. There is a long history of colonialism in the United States where sacred sites and practices have been disrespected or destroyed purposefully. I worry that the killer will strike again on the eve of the crescent moon at the Medicine Wheel. The moon is starting to seem like a symbol of mystery and inevitability. Every time the crescent moon reappears, it foreshadows that another key event or revelation will happen."

"You are starting to think like a profiler," John said. "The moon could also serve as a recurring image that ties together disparate parts of the chaos that the Blood Cresent group wants to create. People interpret the moon differently. Some see it as an omen, others as a comfort, depending on their beliefs."

"I was doing some research last night while feeding the twins, and I discovered that the crescent moon could be tied to an old prophecy or a spiritual leader. The prophet may have foreseen that death would come during this lunar phase. I feel like we are racing against time to try to prevent another Red Hand murder in June at the Medicine Wheel."

"You sound convicted in this resolve. I'm not sure that I buy in this deeply to your conviction, but I am more than willing to hear you out," John said.

Just then, Kate walked into the conference room.

"We are ready for you outside on the courthouse steps. Mac instructed me that she would go first and that she would introduce you to the main interview. Burg just pulled up, and I told him to meet us on the steps," Kate instructed.

They walked out in unison. Mac could feel a growing pit in her stomach.

# Chapter 30

Fear. Denial.    Obsession. The crescent moon evoked different feelings for different people.

# Chapter 31

Patty Ramirez was a middle-aged Native Sioux living in Ranchester, Wyoming, on the outskirts of Sheridan. She called and left a voicemail on Mac's work line explaining that she was experiencing an internal struggle with premonitions, and she sensed that something terrible was about to happen. Her message stated that she was being haunted by visions and nightmares where the crescent moon figures prominently, but she can't interpret its meaning until it's too late. She has certain moments of clarity, but when she goes to write them down, she can't remember them.

Mac was well-versed in the significance of the crescent moon and its meaning to Native Americans through not only folklore but prophecy. Natives were extremely intuitive with nature, and she felt like Patty Ramirez was struggling with the knowledge that she could possibly present a murder. She was likely feeling anxiety, guilt and shame for not being able to articulate her premonition with specificity.

Mac had a growing premonition as well, and an increasing obsession with the moon's symbolism. She was looking for clues in every crescent moon phase. She saw the crescent moon as an omen or a sign of mystery. Burg thought that she was becoming paranoid about it, but he didn't dare tell that to her face. He knew better.

# Chapter 32

Is it just me, or is my concept of a prophecy that is tied to the crescent moon creating the same sense of fatalism as Patty Ramirez? Mac asked John Douglas.

"It's me too," John admitted. "I am coming to grips with the idea that there will be a murder this month at the Medicine Wheel. Like it is written in the stars. Fate," he continued.

"I also feel that this fated event will be worse than before. More brutal in that it will be a vicious attack, and the murder will evade us again," Mac stated with conviction.

"I agree, unfortunately on all accounts. I've even spoken with my boss and long-time colleague at the FBI about it. He thinks that I should calm down. He believes that I get too hyped up about these things," John said.

"Burg thinks that I'm being superstitious. He says that I need to stay neutral and grounded. I wanted to throat punch him, in a loving way, of course," Mac said.

John burst out laughing. Mac joined him. The laughter broke some tension.

"Let's go out for a walk and talk further about this. I feel like getting some fresh air," Mac suggested.

"That sounds solid. I feel like the walls are closing in on us," John said.

# Chapter 33

The crescent moon was set to peak the following evening, and the town was full of whispers and trepidation. Burg, Mac, John, and Kate would be at the Medine Wheel on the perimeter, and Burg had ordered those reinforcements from other Wyoming towns be present to protect the Natives during their most sacred night of the lunar moon. Tribes from all over the United States would be present to worship at the Medicine Wheel, and it was closed to the public the entire month of June to honor Native Americans.

Burg's mother would take care of the twins, as Burg and Mac expected to pull an "all-nighter" on surveillance. The elders of the Native Americans had granted an exception to their rule of no photography or videography, and they granted Kate and other newscasters permission to cover the event for the safety of the Indigenous people.

As crowds of people drove up the Bighorn Mountains to the Medicine Wheel, tensions rose. The tension in town seemed to be taking a psychological toll, as folks were constantly watching the skies for the crescent moon, and it was wearing people down. People who were otherwise kind and respectful were short with each other and overall grouchy.

As crowds gathered to witness the Natives in their ceremonial wear, law enforcement was on the lookout for the Red Hands killer.

# Chapter 34

As the sun rose, there was a collective sign of relief. No one was murdered. Everyone was safe.

"We did it," John said to Mac and Burg. "Whew."

People were fist-bumping and high-fiving as they ventured towards their vehicles. It was as if people had changed gears from being on edge, back to being relaxed and friendly.

Folks waived to one another again on Main Street in downtown Sheridan. Cars let each other pass. People stopped and chatted. People were back to being their normal friendly selves.

Sheridan felt safe again.

# Chapter 35

Mac and Burg had stopped at Java Moon to get strong coffee to get them through the day. John went back to the Historic Sheridan Inn to get some rest, as did Kate.

Mac and Burg still had a killer on the loose, and they were no closer to finding this person or persons. It was disturbing.

When Mac got back to her office, Burg got a call. She watched as his face turned from its normal healthy color to a dull pale gray.

"Where?" Burg shouted into the phone. "You have got to be kidding me," he continued. "We are on the way."

Mac looked at her husband with extreme concern.

"What is going on?" she asked.

"There was a murder last night at Devils Tower. A native woman. Same M.O. Brutal this time. She was stabbed to death 47 times and her red handprint covered her mouth. There is a crosshair insignia on her inner thigh. Red Hand Killer struck at one of the other most sacred Native areas in Wyoming. We were tricked," Burg said.

Tears welled in Mac's eyes. She felt like it was her fault. She never even considered that the perpetrator would know where they would be, and so he or she ventured elsewhere to kill another Indigenous woman in the same manner as was the pattern. She felt deeply haunted and disturbed.

"Get your things and call my mom," Burg commanded. "We have to go to Devils Tower now."

Mac did as she was told and she gathered her things, including the box of files for the Red Hands Killer, and she called Burg's mother, and then John, and then Kate.

They would need to caravan to Devils Tower for an investigation.

# Chapter 36

Devils Tower is a butte, possibly laccolithic, composed of igneous rock in the Bear Lodge Ranger District of the Black Hills, near Hulette and Sundance in Crook County of northeastern Wyoming, above the Belle Fourche River. It rises 1,267 feet above the Belle Fourche River, standing 867 feet from the summit to the base. The summit is 5,112 feet above sea level. It is a national monument in Wyoming.

Devils Tower is a natural feature and has strong spiritual significance to Native Americans. The base of the monolith is surrounded by a boulder field, where large rocks have tumbled down over the centuries. This chaotic, rugged landscape is symbolic, with the rocks almost appearing as remnants of something ancient and powerful, which is tied into Native American folklore.

The trails around Devils Tower pass through wooded sections. The thick forest creates a sense of isolation, with the trees taking on a persona of watchful eyes.

The monument is considered sacred by several Native American tribes, and there are prayer bundles and other sacred items placed around the base.

At nighttime, the tower casts shadows and the sense of the supernatural is amplified. This is why the movie "Close Encounters of the Third Kind" was filmed here. The silhouette of the Tower against the night sky is a powerful image, especially with the crescent moon.

When they arrived at Devils Tower, they were greeted by law enforcement from around the state who escorted them to the scene of the crime.

The yellow crime scene table blew in the wind on the eastern slope of the Tower need to a forested area. The bloody body had been brutalized and then cast aside near a sacred bundle of colorful scarves that were tied to a small pine tree.

She had been identified by family as Sheila SingsWithWolves and she was a member of the Sioux tribe. She was 17 years old and extremely beautiful, with long straight black hair and olive-toned skin gorgeous, deeply set dark eyes and a thin nose. She had a bloody handprint covering her mouth, and her clothes were masked in dark, dry blood.

Mac felt nauseous as she gazed at this lifeless beautiful soul. How cruel did a person need to be to take the life of a lovely young woman with such horrible force? It appeared to be an anger kill. There was no doubt that it was overkill, as no one could survive that many stab wounds.

Mac turned to Kate, who was already crying. Mac was crying too. Burg and John were as well. This scene provoked a reaction. Not a good one.

# Chapter 37

Burg's DNA crew finished their analysis of the crime scene, and there was not one trace of evidence left behind. Not a single trace.

"How are we going to catch this killer if he or she knows how not to leave evidence at the scene?" Mac asked Burg. He shrugged. John just shook his head in dismay.

The psychological impact rippled through the group. They knew that it would also ripple through the Indigenous people as well as all residents of Wyoming and neighboring states.

"It's as if the killer is using the crescent moon as a psychological weapon, taunting us," John said.

"Agreed," Burg echoed.

"He is using it as a supernatural presence, a symbol of fate, fear, and power," Mac suggested. "And we have absolutely no clue who the perpetrator is."

"We may never know who it is," John said. "The Zodiac Killer has haunted me all of my career as an FBI criminal profiler."

"The Red Hands Killer is haunting me in my professional and personal life," Mac said.

# Chapter 38

Mac soon learned to dread the Cresent Moon. The summer went by quickly and without any incident of further Red Hands murders reported. The killer was dormant, but it didn't mean that people weren't leery.

It would be the first case in Mac's career that she ended up empty-handed.